WILD WORK

Who Rolls Through Fire?
WORKING ON A MOVIE SET

Mary Meinking

Chicago, Illinois

www.heinemannraintree.com
Visit our website to find out
more information about
Heinemann-Raintree books.

To order:

☎ Phone 888-454-2279

▣ Visit www.heinemannraintree.com
to browse our catalog and order online.

Edited by David Andrews, Nancy Dickmann, and Rebecca
Rissman
Designed by Victoria Allen
Picture research by Liz Alexander
Leveled by Marla Conn, with Read-Ability.
Originated by Dot Gradations Ltd
Printed and bound in China by Leo Paper Products Ltd

15 14 13 12 11 10
10 9 8 7 6 5 4 3 2 1

Library of Congress Cataloging-in-Publication Data
Meinking, Mary.
 Who rolls through fire? : working on a movie set / Mary
Meinking.
    p. cm.—(Wild work)
 Includes bibliographical references and index.
 ISBN 978-1-4109-3850-3 (hc)—ISBN 978-1-4109-3860-2
(pb) 1. Motion pictures—Vocational guidance—Juvenile
literature. I. Title.
 PN1995.9.P75C43 2010
 791.43023—dc22   2009050285

Acknowledgements
The author and publisher are grateful to the following for
permission to reproduce copyright material:

2005 TopFoto p. 19; Alamy pp. 4 (© Melvyn Longhurst),
6 (© Photos 12), **7** (© Jeff Morgan The Arts), **10** (© AWB
Photography), **13** (© imagebroker), **14** (© Mike Goldwater),
17 (© Jeff Mood), **18** (© JHP Attractions), **20** (© LHB Photo),
21 (© Photos 12), **25** (© eddie linssen), **27** (© Adrian Sherratt);
Corbis pp. **5** (© Christophe d'Yvoire/Sygma), **9** (© Ann
Johansson), **11** (© Francois Duhamel / DREAMWORKS/
Bureau L.A. Collection), **15** (© Luc Roux), **28** (© Luc Roux);
Getty Images pp. **8** (Tom Kingston/WireImage), **12** (Ian
Wingfield), **24** (Doug Allan/The Image Bank), **26** (Warrick
Page); Press Association Images p. **16** (Ted S. Warren/AP);
Rex Features pp. **23** (NBCUPHOTOBANK), **29** (© Magnolia/
Everett); The Kobal Collection p. **22** (Walt Disney Pictures/
Walden Media).

Background design features reproduced with permission
of Shutterstock (© Jenny Horne).

Cover photograph reproduced with permission of Corbis
(© Yuri Kochetkov/epa).

Every effort has been made to contact copyright holders of
any material reproduced in this book. Any omissions will
be rectified in subsequent printings if notice is given to
the publisher.

Disclaimer
All the Internet addresses (URLs) given in this book were valid
at the time of going to press. However, due to the dynamic
nature of the Internet, some addresses may have changed, or
sites may have changed or ceased to exist since publication.
While the author and publisher regret any inconvenience this
may cause readers, no responsibility for any such changes can
be accepted by either the author or the publisher.

J-nf

Some words are shown in bold, **like this**. You can find
out what they mean by looking in the glossary.

Contents

Movie Time. 4

Action! 6

Fame and Fortune. 8

Looking Their Best 12

What a Stunt! 16

All Set? 20

Computer Magic. 22

Roll Film 24

Lights and Sound. 26

Could You Work on a Movie Set? 28

Glossary 30

Find Out More 31

Index 32

Movie Time

Lights, camera, action! Welcome to the movie set. It takes hundreds of people to make a movie. Everyone has a job to do.

Some people act in front of the camera. Even more people work behind the **scenes** to make the movie a success.

Action!

Directors are like storytellers. They turn the words in the **script**, or story, into a movie. They plan each **scene** of the movie.

director

Directors tell the actors what they should be doing in front of the camera. They also direct the light, sound, and camera crews.

Fame and Fortune

Actors need to do more than just remember to say their lines in front of a camera. They make believe they're the **characters** they're playing. Their voice, crooked smile, or limp makes their character seem more real.

DID YOU KNOW?

Famous movie stars have their own movie trailers. They sleep, eat, or change there between **scenes**.

People go to places such as Hollywood, New York, or **Bollywood** in Mumbai, India to get into movies. Only a few become stars. Many become **extras** in group **scenes**.

extras

Some actors are children. They can only act a few hours each day. They have to keep going to school. Teachers come to the set to help them with their homework.

Looking Their Best

Hair **stylists** style actors' hair. They make sure the actor's hair doesn't change from one **scene** to the next.

Makeup artists add crooked noses, bloody cuts, or make actors look much older. Foam is **molded** around actors to look like monsters, aliens or even animals.

Costume designers find or make the clothes used in movies. The clothing must match the time and place of the movie's story. Designers plan what every actor wears, from head to toe.

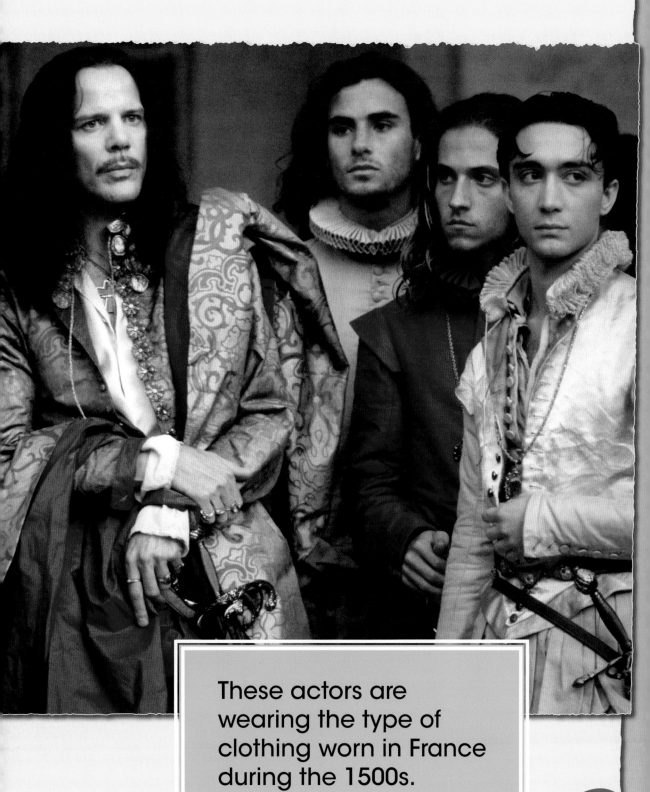

These actors are wearing the type of clothing worn in France during the 1500s.

What a Stunt!

Stunt people take the place of some movie stars for dangerous **scenes**. Stunt people know how to do the stunts safely.

Remember you're not a stunt person, so don't try any of these tricks!

Some stunt people are even set on fire. They put on special clothes under their costumes. They cover their costumes with a liquid that burns without hurting them. But it still can be dangerous!

Stunt people are used when **characters** are in fights or fall. They're needed when cars explode or tumble off a cliff.

DID YOU KNOW?

In a "stunt fight," stunt people stand a few feet apart. One person pretends to punch. The other pretends to get hit. The camera behind them can't see that it wasn't a real punch.

All Set?

The art **department** finds everything that you see in a movie, except for the actors and their costumes. They buy or make the **props** used in each scene. Model makers build tiny buildings, trees, and airplanes.

This model ship and city
look life-sized on camera!

Computer Magic

Computer images show what people can't build. They can make thousands of soldiers, bugs, or space ships. Computers make aliens and monsters look real.

Sometimes actors are filmed
in front of a green screen. Then
a dangerous place is filmed. The
computer combines the two shots.
It looks like the actors are in
that dangerous place.

Roll Film

Camera operators film the movie. There are several cameras filming at the same time. But they film from different places. One of them will get the perfect shot the **director** needs.

They film in all types of weather.
Sometimes they're underwater or
next to a speeding car.

Lights and Sound

People called **gaffers** are in charge of lights. They shine **spotlights** or colored lights on the scenes. Gaffers use huge white cards to bounce light into dark spots.

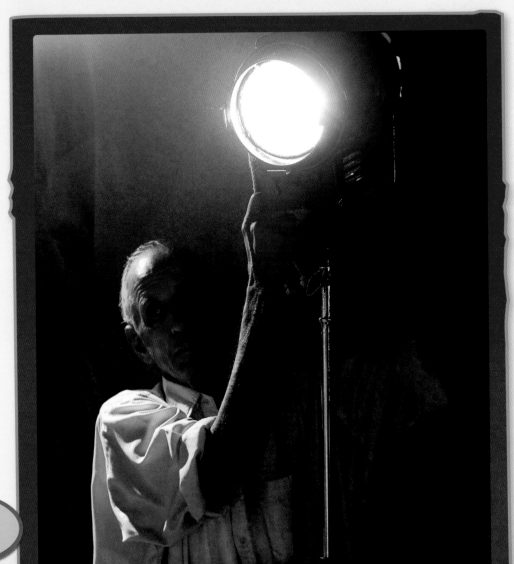

boom
operator

Boom operators hold long-armed **microphones** over the actors. They capture every whisper, grunt, and sneeze. **Sound effects** are added to films to make them sound more real.

Could You Work on a Movie Set?

Everyone on the movie crew must work long and hard. They must like to travel because they could film anywhere in the world.

The movie crew must work together as a team. Everyone wants the movie to be the next big hit!

Glossary

Bollywood the center of India's film business

boom a microphone on a long pole

character person who an actor represents in a movie or play

department group with its own jobs

director person who guides the actors and says how a movie is made

extras background actors who don't speak in movies

gaffer person who does the lighting on a movie set

microphone a devise that captures sound so it can be recorded

molded fitted into a shape

props objects used in a movie

scene part of a movie that is set in one place

script a written play broken down with actor's parts

sound effects made-up sounds

spotlight a strong beam of light shone in one area

stunt a dangerous act done by someone

stylist person who cuts and shapes hair

Find Out More

Books to Read

Friedman, Lise. *Break a Leg! The Kid's Guide to Acting and Stagecraft.* New York: Workman Publishing Company, 2002.

Wessling, Katherine. *Backstage at a Movie Set.* Danbury, CT: Rosen Book Works, Inc., 2003.

Web Site to Visit

http://www.stuntacademy.com/index.html
This site teaches kids how to be stunt people.

Index

actors 5, 7, 8, 9, 10–11,
    12, 13, 14, 23, 27
art department 20

blue screens 23
boom operators 7

camera operators 7,
    24–25
characters 8, 18
child actors 11
computer images 22, 23
costume designers 14
costumes 14, 17

danger 16, 17, 23
directors 6–7, 24

extras 10

gaffers 7, 26

hair stylists 12

makeup artists 13
microphones 27
model makers 20
molds 13
movie stars 9, 10, 16

props 20

scenes 6, 12, 16, 20,
    23, 26
school 11
scripts 6
sound crews 7, 27
sound effects 27
"stunt fighting" 19
stunt people 16–18, 19

team work 29
trailers 9
travel 28